Dear Parent:
Your child's love of reading starts here!

Every child learns to read in a different way and at his or her own speed. Some go back and forth between reading levels and read favorite books again and again. Others read through each level in order. You can help your young reader improve and become more confident by encouraging his or her own interests and abilities. From books your child reads with you to the first books he or she reads alone, there are I Can Read Books for every stage of reading:

SHARED READING
Basic language, word repetition, and whimsical illustrations, ideal for sharing with your emergent reader

BEGINNING READING
Short sentences, familiar words, and simple concepts for children eager to read on their own

READING WITH HELP
Engaging stories, longer sentences, and language play for developing readers

READING ALONE
Complex plots, challenging vocabulary, and high-interest topics for the independent reader

ADVANCED READING
Short paragraphs, chapters, and exciting themes for the perfect bridge to chapter books

I Can Read Books have introduced children to the joy of reading since 1957. Featuring award-winning authors and illustrators and a fabulous cast of beloved characters, I Can Read Books set the standard for beginning readers.

A lifetime of discovery begins with the magical words **"I Can Read!"**

Visit www.icanread.com for information
on enriching your child's reading experience.

I Can Read Book® is a trademark of HarperCollins Publishers.

The Dark Knight Rises: Tools of the Trade
Copyright © 2012 DC Comics.
BATMAN and all related characters and elements are trademarks of and © DC Comics.
(s12)

HARP5004
Printed in the United States of America. No part of this book may be used or reproduced in any manner whatsoever without written permission except in the case of brief quotations embodied in critical articles and reviews. For information address HarperCollins Children's Books, a division of HarperCollins Publishers, 10 East 53rd Street, New York, NY 10022.
www.icanread.com

Library of Congress catalog card number: 2012930071
ISBN 978-0-06-213223-9

Book design by John Sazaklis

12 13 14 15 16   LP/WOR   10 9 8 7 6 5 4 3 2 1
❖
First Edition

I Can Read!

READING WITH HELP 2

THE DARK KNIGHT RISES™

Tools of the Trade

Adapted by Jodi Huelin

Pictures by Steven E. Gordon

Colors by Eric Gordon

INSPIRED BY THE FILM THE DARK KNIGHT RISES
SCREENPLAY BY JONATHAN NOLAN AND CHRISTOPHER NOLAN
STORY BY CHRISTOPHER NOLAN AND DAVID S. GOYER
BATMAN CREATED BY BOB KANE

HARPER
An Imprint of HarperCollinsPublishers

It is my headquarters, my lab,
and my training room.
Only my closest friend and loyal butler,
Alfred, knows where it is.

To fight crime, I need to have
the most high-tech equipment.
For that, I depend on Lucius Fox.
He works for Wayne Enterprises.

Lucius created
the Batsuit and all
the tools I carry on
my Utility Belt.

Lucius created the Tumbler, too.

It is an all-terrain vehicle.

I painted it all black and

gave it a new name:

the Batmobile!

It helps me go just about anywhere.

Lucius shows me a new invention.

It is called the Bat.

It can fly in-between buildings.

It can also hover in one place.

Bad guys had better beware!

I rely on the Batcomputer for information.

It helps me track bad guys.

It can analyze chemicals.

It can even scan fingerprints.

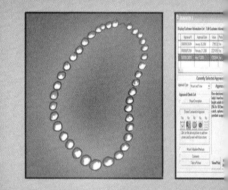

When someone broke into my house
and stole my mother's necklace,
it identified the thief instantly.
Catwoman!

Using a tracking device

on the necklace,

I trace Catwoman to a party.

To catch her,

I leave the Batsuit behind.

Instead, I go as my alter ego,

billionaire Bruce Wayne.

I dance with Catwoman.

I take the necklace back.

Back at the Batcave, I learn that criminals have broken into the stock exchange building.
I jump on the Bat-Pod.
It is a fast and sleek motorcycle.
It travels quickly through the narrow streets of Gotham City.

I arrive at the
Gotham City Stock Exchange—
and just in time!

The criminal's name is Bane.

He's the newest bad guy in town.

Bane wants to destroy Gotham City.

He will stop at nothing to do it.

Bane and his henchmen

knocked out the security guards.

They didn't want money.

They wanted information.

The gang escapes from the stock exchange!

They zoom away on their motorcycles.

I zoom after them on the Bat-Pod.

I pull out another new gadget.

It is my EMP rifle.

It fires an electromagnetic pulse

that saps the energy out of any machine.

When I get close enough,

I take steady aim and fire.

ZAP!

The pulse kills their engines.

Their motorcycles sputter and crash.

But it's not over yet.

The criminals want to fight.

I am an expert in martial arts.

I've had years of training.

I'm always ready

for anything

or anyone.

Minutes later, the police arrive.

They're just in time to haul

these bad guys off to jail.

But Bane is missing!

He must have escaped during the fight.

I cannot let him get away.

Bane's headquarters are deep underground.

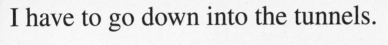

I have to go down into the tunnels.

I will find him wherever he is hiding.

In order to keep Gotham City safe,

I always rely on several things.

My amazing tools and powerful vehicles

make me a master crime fighter.

Criminals beware!